The Somebody Kid

BY
CHARLOTTE GRAEBER
ILLUSTRATED BY
JOE BODDY

Thomas Nelson Publishers
Nashville • Camden • New York

"I'm tired of being nobody!" I said one morning as I stood in front of the bathroom mirror. Every day at school somebody got attention. Joe told jokes and everyone laughed. Mike made the most points in kick ball. Yesterday my sister even got an award for spelling.

But nobody ever noticed me. I splashed water on the mirror. "Today I am going to be *somebody!*"

Published in Nashville, Tennessee, by Thomas Nelson, Inc. and distributed in Canada by Lawson Falle, Ltd., Cambridge, Ontario.

Printed in the United States of America.

ISBN: 0-8407-6640-8

Usually I sit at the front of the room. But not today. Today I plopped into a seat at the back.

"Why aren't you in your own seat?" the teacher asked.

"I take my own seat with me," I said and pointed to the back of my jeans. All of the kids laughed. I laughed too.

"Are you sick?" the teacher asked. She marched me to my own desk. I felt good.

For gym we went outside. Every day I sit on the sidelines. But not today. Today I grabbed the football and kicked it hard--right over the fence.

Some of the kids laughed. I laughed too.

"What's wrong with you?" the gym teacher asked.
He made me go after the ball.
But I felt good. I felt good all
morning. Everyone was
starting to notice me.

After lunch we had a surprise test in math. I copied the smartest kid's paper. He'd sat right beside me all year, but I *never* did that before. I know I got most of the problems right.

Dad would notice that!

Just as the bell rang, the intercom crackled. "Attention!" the principal said. "Mr. T is coming to our school! Grades one through three report to the gym at two o'clock! Everyone else at three o'clock!"

We all hollered and stamped our feet. Everone likes Mr. T. We all watch him on TV. This was my chance to be somebody *big*!

But how?

I could get Mr. T's autograph. I could get his picture. But all the kids would do that. Somehow I had to make everyone—

—even Mr. T!

—notice me.

At two o'clock
we hurried to the gym.
We sat down on the bleachers.
At last Mr. T arrived. His gold
chains flashed. His combat boots
echoed on the wooden floor.
Everyone cheered.

Then I saw Mr. T's socks. One sock was green. One sock was bright yellow. I waited until the yelling stopped. Then I jumped up. "Hey, Mr. T, you got two different socks on!" I yelled and sat down. Some of the kids laughed. Others sat quietly. After all, who messes with Mr. T!

Mr. T glared at the bleachers. He looked directly at me. So I jumped up again. "One sock green, one sock yellow!" I chanted. "Mr. T, are you blind or something?" This time most of the kids laughed. After all, Mr. T *was* wearing two odd socks.

I looked around. Now I had everyone's attention. I was
SOMEBODY!

Mr. T pointed a finger right at me. "You want to mess with Mr. T?" he shouted. He climbed the bleachers two at a time.

My teacher was beside me. She pulled on my elbow. "Sit down! Sit down *now*!" she ordered.

Mr. T waved her away. "We got to get to the bottom of this!" He put his hand on my shoulder. "Out with it! What's bothering you?"

I wiped my hands on my knees. The whole school was watching. NOBODY messes with Mr. T—especially when he's got you by the shoulder.

"I wanted to be somebody," I said. Mr. T's knuckles bumped my ear. I didn't feel so good.

Mr. T leaned down. "You ain't goin' to be somebody puttin' other people down. Nobody needs to prove themselves.

You *already* is somebody. Don't you know that?"

"How can I be somebody?" I asked. "Nobody ever pays attention to me!"

"You just got to be yourself! God made you somebody!" Mr. T said. "He likes you just the way you are . . . and He likes *me* just the way I am—odd socks and all. I don't try to please anybody but Him!"

He looked around the gym. "We *all*

somebody, right?" "Right!" everyone hollered back.

Mr. T climbed to the top seats. He pointed to kids, one at a time.

"Only one you!" he said. "Only one me!"

"Only one you!" we all shouted back. "Only one me!"

The kids crowded in for Mr. T's autograph.

But he signed my notebook first.

"To Mr. Somebody," he wrote,

"from Mr. T."

Phonics Reading Program

SO-AHF-212
Book 4
short o

Hop Like a Tree Frog!

by Quinlan B. Lee

SCHOLASTIC INC.

New York   Toronto   London   Auckland   Sydney
Mexico City   New Delhi   Hong Kong   Buenos Aires

The red-eyed tree **frogs** need our help!
The **frogs** are **on** a **log** going down the river.
The **log** will **not stop**.

The wind is making the
ChaCha Coconut Trees
drop their coconuts.
Hop like a tree **frog**
so they will **not drop on** us!
Hop, hop, hop!

Do you **spot** the tree **frogs**?
There they are!
We must **stop** the **log**!
It is going into the pyramid.

Do you **spot** the door?
Look! It is at the **top**.
How can we get to the **top**?
I have gloves that stick
like tree **frog** toes.

We can climb to the **top**
like a tree **frog**.
Hop on, Baby Jaguar.
Let's climb to the
top, **top**, **top**!

Now do you **spot** the tree **frogs**?
Quick! We must **stop** the **log**.
We do **not** have a **lot** of time!

Tree **frogs**, **hop** off your **log** to the **top** of this **rock**. **Hop, hop, hop!** **Hop** to this **rock**!

We **got** the tree **frogs**!